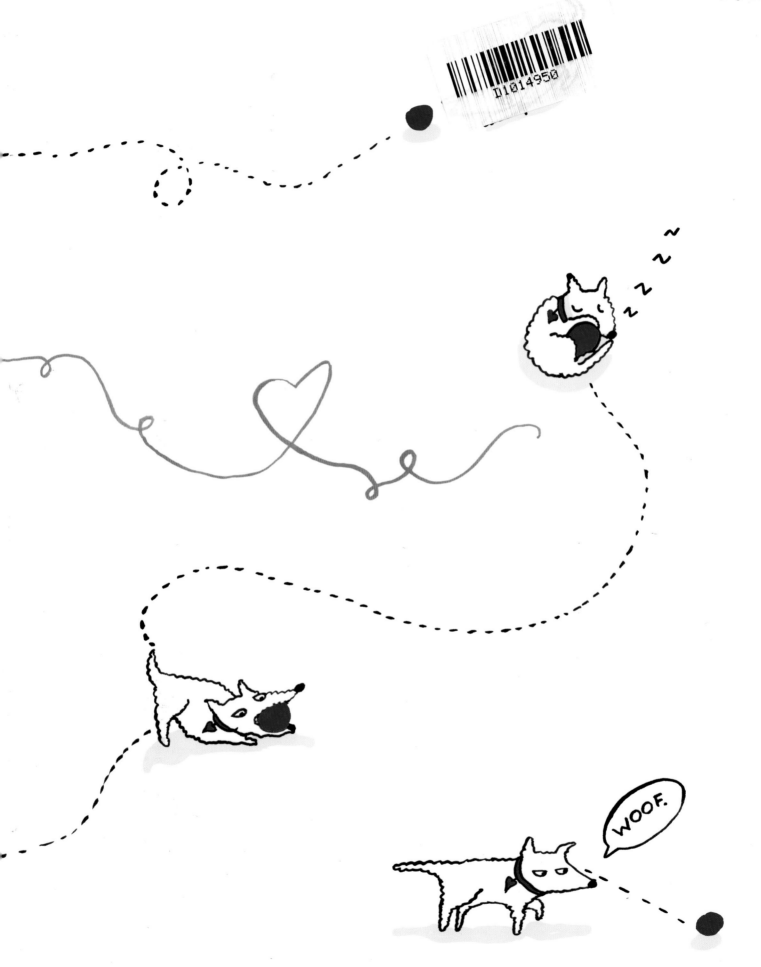

to Christina

First edition 2017

Published by Peter Pauper Press, Inc.
202 Mamaroneck Avenue
White Plains, New York 10601 USA

Published in the United Kingdom and Europe
by Peter Pauper Press, Inc.
c/o White Pebble International
Unit 2, Plot 11 Terminus Rd.
Chichester, West Sussex PO19 8TX, UK

Library of Congress Cataloging-in-Publication Data Available

ISBN 978-1-4413-2287-6

Manufactured for Peter Pauper Press, Inc.
Printed in Hong Kong

7 6 5 4 3 2 1

Visit us at www.peterpauper.com

ROSIE AND CRAYON

DEBORAH MARCERO

 Peter Pauper Press, Inc.
White Plains, New York

Rosie loved her pup, Crayon.

And Crayon L O V E D Rosie.

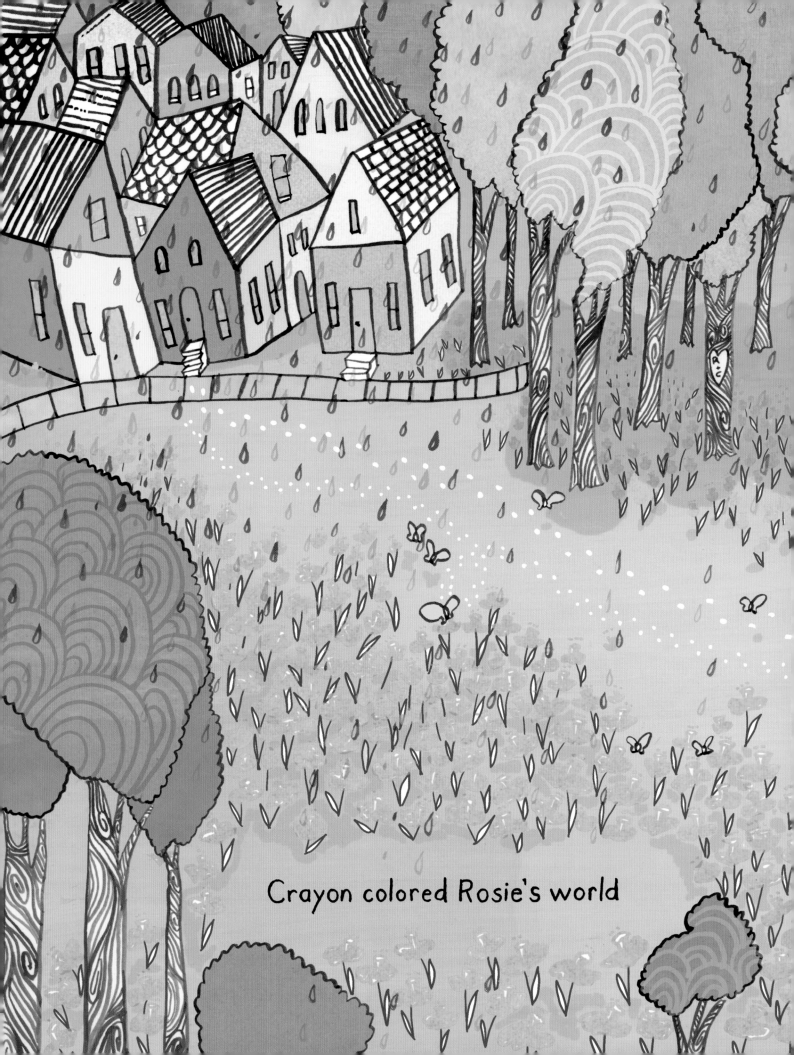

Crayon colored Rosie's world

with tickled greens
and fluttering yellows.

With simmering reds and oranges that smoldered into pink.

With every shade that blue
could ever imagine.

Even with darker hues
like licorice, onyx,

and purples so deep they could only
belong to midnight.

Until one day, after a long and colorful life,
Crayon was gone.

The sky filled with clouds
that pinched out the sun.

Black became suitable.
White worked like an eraser.
And gray could mask almost anything.

Rosie's heart zipped itself up,
and the world became a cold, colorless place.

LOST
LOST
INKY!
INKSTER!
INKYYY!
HERE KITTY!
LOST
MISSING : KITTEN
Goes by the name of INKY,
INKSTER OR INK-A-LICIOUS
Loves sunsets and bouncy balls
call
LOST

For the first time without Crayon,
Rosie felt like taking a walk.

She kept watch for the little black kitten. Once in a while, she even whispered,

inky

come here inkster

here kitty, kitty

Rosie searched and searched,
through the neighborhood,
beyond the woods,

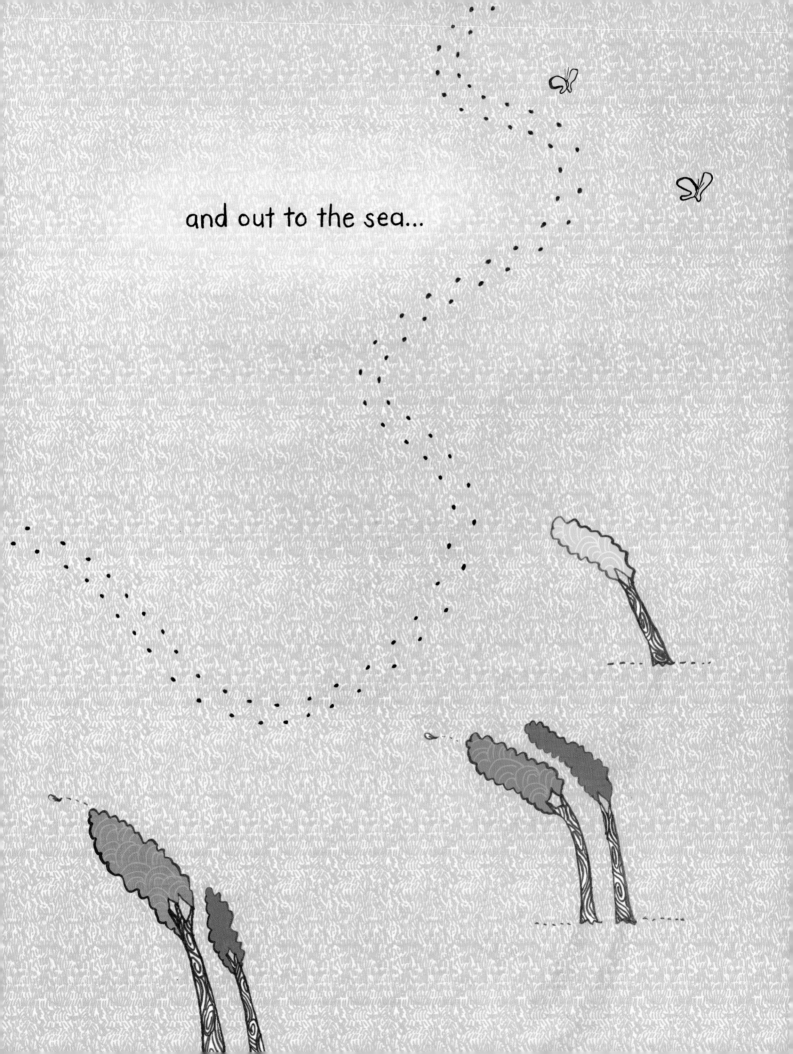

and out to the sea...

...where finally, near sunset,
a speck of hope
shivered on the horizon.

Rosie let herself remember Crayon.

Rosie's tears reflected all the colors that filled her world.

The gray wash of the waves slowly became
green, yellow, red, orange, pink, blue
and a purple so deep it could only belong to midnight.

 Rosie's heart didn't break
(like she thought it would). Rather...

...it felt wider — taller — deeper
than it had ever felt before.

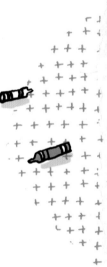